BY JACK W AND CHARLIE FINN

WITH SAPPHIRE DESIGNS.CO.UK

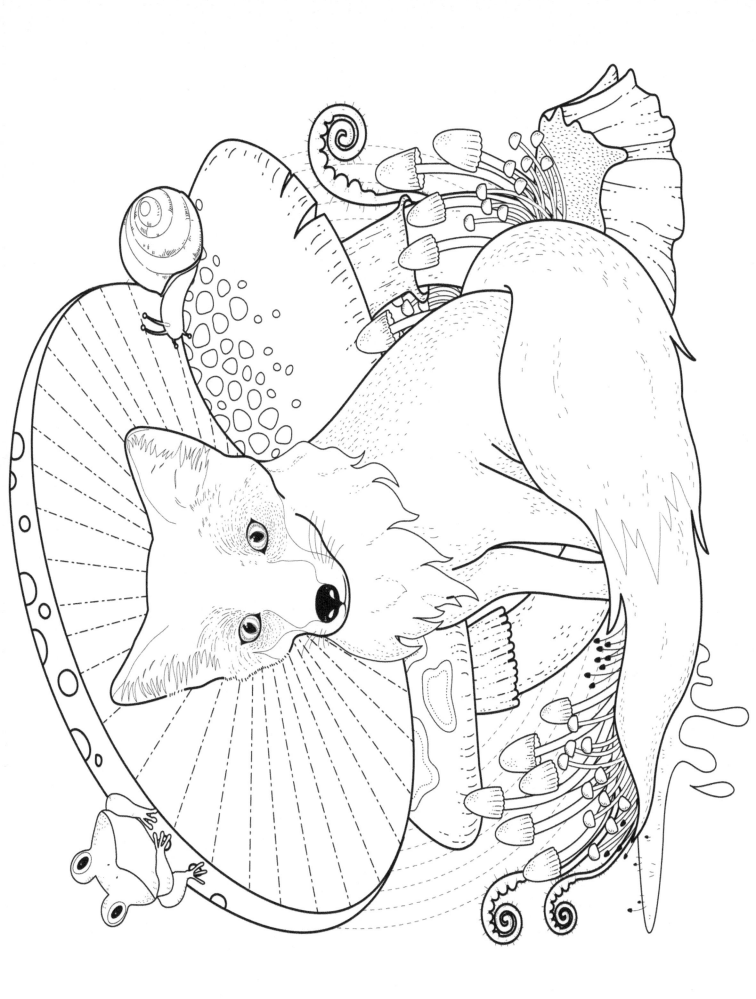

happiness is...

PEN TEST

USE THIS AREA TO TEST OUT YOUR PENS

PEN TEST

USE THIS AREA TO TEST OUT YOUR PENS

PEN TEST

USE THIS AREA TO TEST OUT YOUR PENS

THE FUN DOESNT HAVE TO END HERE!
JUST BEHIND THIS PAGE IS AN EXCLUSIVE
FIRST LOOK AT OUR NEXT COLOURING BOOK...

PIG MANIA

COMING SOON

CHARLIE FINN | JACK W FINN

WITH SAPPHIREDESIGNS.CO.UK

THE STORY BEHIND THE COLOURING BOOK

Freya Fox thought she was going to have the best seven birthday party that all the foxes of Foxes Cove had ever seen.

But unfortunately for Freya, that's when disaster stuck! Swept away during a game of hide and seek by a huge thunderstorm, she wakes up in a strange place that's not her home.

Lost and frightened, Freya is found by a piglet called Pip, who has the heart of a brave lion.

Now Freya with the help of Pip must journey across the sea and into unknown places to help her find her way back home.

* Freya Fox's Big Birthday Adventure is a short complete bedtime story written by a fox obsessed seven-year-old Jack and his mother Charlie.

Made in the USA
Middletown, DE
10 July 2019